AF485867

DOG SYMPOSIUM

POEMS

ZORAN JUNGIC

Edited by
ANNELIES WEISER

Copyright © 2021 by ZORAN JUNGIC

All rights reserved.

No part of this book may be reproduced in any form or by any electronic or mechanical means, including information storage and retrieval systems, without written permission from the author, except for the use of brief quotations in a book review.

❋ Created with Vellum

Contents

WRONG NUMBER

At the glass edge
    Exiled birds kneel and pray
    While we quarrel with our next-door neighbors
    In the early spring
    Leaving the warm darkness behind
    Ready to swim across
    The burning river at dawn
    And set up the trap
    For each other
    In the land where nothing grows
    Where only some orphans are
    Still falling from the sky
    Into the weed overgrown
    Sea.

GLASS OF POISON

She was inhaling and exhaling the sick air
    Thinking of her childhood
    When she would catch the first train north
    To be as far as she could from the war
    But now
    She kept asking herself over and over
    What has she achieved now
    What has she written in the books
    Faded away a long time ago
    What has she given to others
    To help them
    While the invisible sandglass
    Was filling fast with ruins
    At this late hour
    When not many dared to kiss
    The remnants
    Of her ash-filled bed.

FLOODS BEFORE LANDSLIDES

Despite the sudden change
    In the weather
    The river still raged
    Gnawing at our roots
    And distant bloodlines
    Forcing small insects
    To hide in the lair
    Where two entwined bodies
    Now only skin and bones
    Continued to disintegrate
    Not paying attention at all
    To their everchanging temper and the past:
    They were just another exhausted pair
    Of cadavers in love
    Sweaty and breathless
    In the middle of the summer afternoon.

WHEN THE BEASTS
TAKE OVER

When was the last time
    We glanced
    From our cell
    At the masked mortals
    Marching down the road
    Happily whispering
    And scratching the pavement
    As if they owned the world.

MEANWHILE
    Somewhere deep inside our neighborhood
    The woman you thought
    Had licked your bones clean
    Suddenly stopped in her tracks
    Looked up
    And smiled.

DAILY EXERCISE

We climbed
    The tree
    Hoping to hear our ancestors
    And perhaps learn something new from them.

THE WINDS CAME to blows
    Reminding us of the barbarian hordes.

PAST MISTAKES

We tried in vain
　　To dive into the weed-adorned waters
　　And to breathe
　　Underneath the wrinkled body of the ocean
　　Turned inside out
　　By the angry waves
　　All those lascivious octopuses.

BUT IF THE tide
　　Hadn't swallowed us
　　That day
　　We would have still been stranded
　　And entangled
　　On coarse tongues of sand
　　Remembering with melancholy
　　Our own
　　Awkward immaculate conception.

ESCAPING NATURE

At early dawn
    When our ears were still black
    From dreams we have been avoiding
    For ages
    And after searching with our eyes
    All night long
    Someone barked above the bed
    Close to the ceiling.

GET your hands up
    Spit out your confession
    Before the colors clash
    And fade away
    When you quickly forget who you are
    Who we were
    Who they were.

. . .

JUST A SPECK of dust managed to escape
From translucent lungs
While the blood-thirsty hyenas were just waking up
Inside our gentle breast.

IT'S ALL THE SAME AS BEFORE

The pear trees
    In the courtyard
    Suffered stoically
    Under the raining artillery
    While the hanged soldiers were
    One by one
    Falling off
    The metal branches
    And collecting in the trenches like leaves.

IN THE EARLY autumn
    Their torn apart faces were visible
    And still shamelessly exposed
    To the sun.

NAME AND RANK
    Didn't mean anything
    In that nightmare of boring

Wars
Long ago
The meaning of any given word was crystal clear
Including every single pronounced
Symbol
Despite the end
When the readers
Forgot it all and absolved every single man
Who had happened to pass by.

ONLY WHEN WE began sharing
    Our common language
    With shamans
    Could we dream again
    The slowed-down currents
    Of desert sand
    And the cry of a strangled child
    Appeared only as a warning
    Wrapped in the skin of some other world beyond
    Where the sobered-up jackals
    Suddenly glanced at the sky
    Praying for salvation
    For which it was too late
    And the meaning of the word was
    Already lost forever.

THERE WAS NOTHING MORE TO ADD

THE EYES of the archangel opened wide
    Above the stranded bodies of the exiles
    Waiting patiently in double columns
    Sentenced to an infinite thirst by the river

          · · ·

BEFORE ANYONE COULD HELP them
    Their blue lips parted
    An incredible deluge of words
    Threatening every single breath inside the gills.

WHEN the heavenly messengers
    Flew in
    Announcing the world
    Already known to all
    It was too late then
    For all those passengers to disappear into some sort of
    Nervous speech
    Known only to them
    Or to pretend to ignore
    The cosmic landslides
    Forcing them to surrender.

MUTE and in panic
    The four headless horsemen of the apocalypse continued
    To race and stumble over the course
    Of the true believers
    Galloping in
    Desperately seeking shelter
    Beyond the clouds of their shared past.

IT WASN'T a question of a Kabbalah
    Because it was crystal clear now
    They would never
    Awaken again
    Despite the barely perceptible signs
    Of their inevitable repeated birth.

RATIONS OF LAUGHTER

Our hard-earned imprisonment
    In the sand dunes
    Without growth and form
    Had continued as it should.

AVOIDING tears
    We were aware that we would never again
    Cross the threshold
    Separating us
    From the temple
    Where the shamans feed on fire
    Spitting out words of judgment
    Beneath
    The fragile branches of plane trees.

WE'VE EVEN MANAGED to skip the last century
    Without a trace of bitter longing

Or a reminder of our discarded skin
Stretched now across the pavement
Where it is drying now
In the sunshine of a problematic summer.

TORRENTS AND PRAYERS

Whoever demanded
    Our immediate exposure
    To this inflamed christening
    Under the clouds of tedious pagan arrows
    Must have been desperate to see us hanging
    In the middle of the town square
    Where we remained until further notice
    Accidently conceived
    In the last century
    With our golden teeth still gracing
    The surrounding heavenly hyenas and temples.

NO ONE SAID
    That we've had dreamt all of it
    The entire outer world
    Under the siege of the exploding words.

WHO KNOWS if we will ever pronounce

The same symbols again
In our house of ashes
Understanding their true meaning only
When the penitents force their way from everywhere
Pouring the currents of pain into our deaf ears.

THE MONUMENTS in the park
Continue to be replaced by glass trees
Before which the bearded vultures prayed
And the telephone poles were still adorned
With the rebellious citizens
Who persistently tried to prove while swaying in the wind
That reality could sometimes
Easily slip away
Without any trace of enthusiasm and flair.

BLOOD WAS NOWHERE TO BE SEEN

She folded her arms
    Under her head
    On the hand-embroidered pillow
    Gazing through the ceiling at the myriad of stars
    Scattered randomly
    Across the dusty universe
    Which was suddenly before her.

HER ANCESTOR'S bones were stored
    In the attic
    Where the spider's web and oblivion
    Imprisoned her name too
    Which she still pronounced with difficulty
    While in that sunken bed
    She felt relaxed now
    Passionately inhaling the scent of pine needles
    Left forgotten
    On Chronos' sticky tongue.

DROWNED IN THE MAGIC SPRING

If they could only be awake
    Under those fragile rocks and clouds
    Their fingers and limbs uncut
    Bodies magically intertwined
    Their world would be again as it was before
    And the wind would stop chewing
    All those darkened columns of exiles.

MEANWHILE THE BRIGANDS lurked
    In the perfect silence of a sleepy grove
    Where the squirrels were competing
    In stealing their war medals
    When the past always depended
    On someone who told stories around the fire
    While a nearby brook quickly flowed out
    From the source
    And impatient bursts of foam
    Splashed the leaves on the faces

Of the conspirators
Whose time stopped a long time ago
When the Earth stopped turning
Sinking ever deeper into the abyss
Not remembering anything anymore.

THE MIRROR WAS THE
FIRST TO SHATTER

T

DAYS full of glass mud were before us
   An obscure mass of rocks and sand
   While we still forged forward
   Biting our precious breath
   Pretending to be mute and courageous
   Despite the hunters already catching up with us
   And the whole fragile world crumbling around us
   With the persistent reminder
   Of her
   Who wasn't there anymore
   Of her
   Who didn't write her name in the sand anymore
   But instead
   She floated
   Forever brave
   Between Night and Day
   Where she always felt good

When we were also convinced
That we won't cry anymore
Never wake up
In tears.

BUT THERE IS NOWHERE to go now
We only stand here
Naked and barefoot
Watching
While she sends her last smile
Towards Thanatos
Who still waits patiently
Under her balcony.

STOP THE CARAVANS, STOP THE RAVENS

The underground
    Smells of fog
    Deep in its insides.

UP above
    On a thin surface
    The caravans float downstream
    Forgetting how to cross the river:
    They will never make it to the city
    On time
    And remember the past
    Once and for all.

A little more time is still needed
    One more lifetime
    Is needed
    To heal the bodies in the desert

If only the ravens
Would remain silent.

THEORY OF SURVIVAL

In a ruined temple
     The runaways scratch their faces
     Stubbornly stealing the eyes off the fading walls.

IT'S all good
     The weather is improving
     And the rain has stopped stabbing small girls in tears
     Who will now approach the forest clearing
     And count the bones of their ancestors
     With their backs turned against them.

BUT LOOK
     The edge of the forest has fallen to ruin now
     Where the communal necropolis once hid
     They're dead
     While they drank the magic potion
     Which would bring them life for a moment.
                         .   .   .

PERHAPS EVEN THOSE leprous travelers will
  Suddenly sober up and fly away.

LOOKING FOR THE MINOTAUR

In the hidden labyrinth
    Our luck was in question.

WE STUMBLED on a secret path
    Overgrown in thorns
    Like the rock-strewn Calvary
    Leading to our home.

THEY SANG odes to the Minotaur
    In the long columns
    Garlands were thrown at the passersby
    And after all
    This was in the twenty-first century
    When no one dared to say a wrong word.

TO BE without words

Was the same as being without breath
But even that doesn't matter.

AT THE ALTAR the Minotaur lay dead already
    Strangled
    And covered with a sprinkling of flowers.

SOUNDS OF BABYLON

.

WE JUMPED QUICKLY
    Across the roofs
    Before the ramparts of words
    Collapsed and darkened.

IT WAS a sudden end
    To one of our better intentions
    But this wasn't so important now:
    There is no chance of meeting anyone we know
    To greet.

MEANWHILE
    The city satraps were watching us
    With suspicion
    Just waiting to turn our fragile lives

Upside down.

THERE WAS no escape for us
    No remorse
    Just ruins of right
    Noble words
    Repeated again and again
    In vain.

ONLY THE UNFAITHFUL hunters were left
    To continue circling around us
    Without any personal regret.

RIVERS OF ASH AND SONG

We noticed her only as a shadow
    But it was already too late:
    She flew off quickly
    Grabbing the air with her fingernails
    Silently refusing to hear
    The rebellion
    Against illusory nature
    Below her.

WE COULDN'T MOVE ANYWHERE
    Except to dive under the thin surface of the river
    And inhale sand
    Together with the excited school of fish
    Swallowing the poisoned waters
    And gnawing on our aged faces.

SHE DIDN'T MAKE IT
ON TIME

She lay in the grass
     Counting snakes and stars
     Not noticing the spring morning
     Hovering in the air above her:
     She never thought then
     That one day we would lick
     The dew off her tongue
     And afterward
     Hide in the neighborhood.

BUT THIS WASN'T the first nor the last time
     When the two cadavers in love had been wrestling
     And pinning each other to their bed
     Remaining still
     On the strand
     From the broken armadas had sailed
     Long ago
     Destroying the world the way it was once.

                    .   .   .

IT'S ALL CLEAR NOW:
    This was just a myth after all
    Repeating itself every time
    When we'd run out of words
    Or the insatiable hunger overcoming us the prisoners:

OR IS it only the past
    We don't dare look in the eye.

PASSION OF BUTTERFLIES

They flew and disappeared
    Into the brightness of the day.

THIS HAPPENED in the ruins
    Of the most beautiful summers we rescued from our past.

BUT WHEN WE took a closer look
    It was a sight to behold:

BILLIONS OF PEOPLE open their mouths
    And sing
    Fighting for air.

HISTORY OF A DISAPPEARANCE

We tried to hide
　　And exchange a few unsaid words
　　In a hideout under our city:
　　We couldn't disappear
　　Because of the pack of insatiable memories
　　Stubbornly following the scent of blacked-out stars.

MEANWHILE
　　The wild beasts
　　Stuck to the main road
　　Never resting
　　Never embellishing parts
　　Of their war past.

WHEN WE FINALLY FOUND THE time to count
　　All our victories and defeats
　　The earthly globe leaned heavily

Without mercy
And if we didn't find our way
Quickly
Who knows
Where we would be now.

ALL OTHER SUMMERS

Pure snow would rarely fall
    In our humble room
    Although we always thought
    That the winter might last forever.

THIS WAS a dream of those who were never born
    Announcing their final arrival
    On the day
    When our love nest became
    Full of
    The courageous fear
    Only known to us.

YOU COULD SAY A LOT

The sun was rolling lazily down our backs
    While we stubbornly climbed
    Over there
    Where
    The skeletal remains of a temple
    Patiently incited us
    And waited.

IT WAS our first time
    In front of the Athenian ruins:
    Pressed by the weight of ages
    We thought humbly now
    About dust and fallen rocks
    Exposed to the blows
    Of a recently freed Aegean wind.

LUCKILY
    We managed to avoid the dead

All those pale bones
Of the ancient master builders
Marked by rows
Of insignificant words
Etched in that airless world.

THE TORN off heads of philosophers continued
    To roll down the Acropolis
    Rushing somewhere towards the silence and peace of a park
    Where they will be able to wag their tongues
    And explain the world
    To divine cats and dogs
    While lazily stretching in the sun
    Before the bare feet of that beautiful goddess
    Armed with a bow
    With no arrow.

WHEN WE'D SUDDENLY TURNED around
    We noticed the hordes of quarreling gods and goats
    Descending nosily
    Down the blood-soaked
    Steps of Plaka.

NEVER TIME FOR MEMORIES

WE WATCHED a blind man
    Crash
    Headlong
    Against the tree
    Not far from the necropolis
    Where the hyenas were guarding the entrance
    Laughing at us.

. . .

IF IT WEREN'T for his white cane
       We wouldn't even have known
       What it was all about:

WAS he still embracing the tree
       Waiting for the leaves to fall
       Or was he stubbornly sending messages
       Advising us
       To go back where he came from.

SOMEHOW, WE'VE ALL TURNED INTO ASHES

She was so beautiful
    Gorgeous
    Fearing God
    Only
    When it
    Suited her most.

LATER we never dared
    To disturb
    Whatever was left of her
    And to remind her
    Of our life together
    Before that perfect storm.

WAS IT ALL WORTH IT

The world always expects forgiveness
    Or some sort of a love challenge
    But instead
    It rained all-day
    In our neighborhood
    Reminding us
    Of our oath
    Given a long time ago:

TO STAY dry
    And always in sound mind
    We find a shelter.

ON THOSE UNKNOWN ROCKS

We discovered the holy man
    Quite by accident
    Seeing him in fact as a mirage
    While he unconsciously hovered
    Above the hillside cemetery
    Laughing at us.

HE PAUSED for a moment
    To understand better our lascivious minds
    And to warn us in a whisper
    That he would sooner or later manage
    To elicit a confession
    Of guilt
    From us
    The perfect believers.

WAS IT BEFORE OR AFTER

Only the girls' laughter flashed in the sun now
    Right before our eyes
    Bound with the silk ribbons of awakening
    At dawn
    When our gaze was still recovering
    From the memories.

IT JUST HAPPENED that we were still roaming
    Along the poison-filled river
    Joining the spring flood
    Not able
    To move our gentle limbs
    Stuck in the sand
    Where our loneliness
    And false promises
    Always disturbed accidental swimmers.

WE'VE STILL REMAINED aware

That one day
White galleys of exiles will sail out into the open seas
And the wish not to deconsecrate the lighthouses
Will become crystal clear to everyone
When the false horizon before us
Sinks into the abyss
Of our homeland.

NOTING DOWN THE
ESCAPED WORDS

Despite all grievous bodily harm
    Our planet had inflicted on us
    For some time
    We've always remained
    Loyal to the past
    Guarding the ramparts of our lair
    Breaking teeth against the rock
    Biting the words
    In the mud
    Which had always belonged to someone else anyway.

WE WERE KNOWN EVERYWHERE
    For hiding the language from our children
    We were unique martyrs
    Steeped
    In innocence
    And the belief in the fraternal carnage.

. . .

WE ARE NOT ashamed to admit
    Our mortal sins
    Or to remain
    In the place of departure
    Where time
    Simply stops and forgets.

SURVIVING both the night and our first love
    The post-mortem of our innocence
    Never took place again
    Only the snow drifted and piled up
    Above the graves
    Still warm from sleep.

AND THERE WAS ONLY one message
    Left for the world:
    One lovely sunny day you will
    Inhale darkness
    And exhale sand.

THE SHORTCUT WAS QUICKER

TRIBES AT WAR
    And only later would they cover themselves with green ashes
    And disappear into exile
    With their names erased
    From the walls of a nearby temple
    Postponing their confessions
    Until tomorrow:
    The heavens would finally fall
    When the end of the world had
    Coughed them up already.

ALL THREATS WERE
IN VAIN

In our lives we often clashed
    With various planets
    While our neighbors continued to
    Conspire against us.

ONE SPRING DAY
    Venus and Mars begged us
    To offer them a glass of water
    But we played dumb
    Still preoccupied
    With other
    Promises
    Only known to us.

FORTUNATELY
    That blind old man
    Happened to come by
    Showing us the right way.

IT WAS SOMETHING ELSE

Forget your cracked forehead
    Forget the world never
    Owed you anything
    Anyway
    Simply look into your own
    Eyes
    And repent.

IT WAS NEVER a case of you
    Becoming an angel
    Overnight
    But of you finally accepting
    The song of songs
    Inside a deserted
    Earthly paradise.

IT WAS YOUR TURN

Our tongues were covered with blisters
    Still licking the invisible rope
    Which is sliding gingerly
    Down the hanging
    Tree.

YOU WILL PROBABLY SAY NOW
    We've deserved it all along
    For this lovely countryside to hate us
    And sentence us to be punished
    With eternal repentance
    For all those deeds
    Which we couldn't recall.

A VAMPIRE ON THR
THRESHOLD

His head lay on the stone remaining still
     Despite the persistent
     Last death rattle
     Which had disturbed
     The evil mutes
     During the mass
     In the sensitive phases of the moon.

NO DOUBT
     The whole scene had been obviously staged
     While the knees cracked against the temple floor
     And the bells rang
     All the way to the heavens.

IT WAS a rare resurrection
     Enjoyed by the whole confused
     World

Witnessing the beast
Tearing up
The transparent shroud of gold
With his sharp teeth.

ONLY WITHERED
FLOWERS AND SHADOWS

Her mouth filled with lethargy
    She bravely exited
    The lair
    Leaving behind
    The world
    Where the poets of old were usually dreaming
    Next to each other
    In the sand
    In their poems
    And the singing
    In the last words
    After which they would probably never
    Wake up again.

SIMPLE CONSPIRACY

The colors of spring
    And colorful sounds of blossoms
    Force the insatiable seers
    To tell us the truth
    At last.

UNDER THE OLIVE trees
    The edge of abyss stood
    Trodden by the flock of birds
    Hesitant before taking off
    To face the unforgiving
    Cosmic landscape
    While we were still conspiring in secret
    Ready to expose
    Once more
    The arms
    Bared up to our elbows.

· · ·

DOG SYMPOSIUM

A NEED TO SURVIVE

We've been left as poor orphans
    On the deck of a sunken
    Roman galley
    Deep down
    In the ocean's entrails
    While mutiny was still taking place
    Among the waves:
    It didn't help at all
    That the barbarian echelons
    Continued waiting patiently
    Somewhere nearby
    To adopt us
    Without
    Any word of explanation.

FREE OF DESIRE

It was left to the mob
    Meandering along the city boulevards
    To decide
    Whether go or not
    And attack nearby classic columns and black trees.

PLACARDS AND SLOGANS
    Exposed to the piercing rain bullets
    Shivered like fragile toys
    Before being blown to pieces
    And there was never enough
    Depleted uranium
    When we most needed it
    Hopefully to halt
    The hordes
    Persistently pushing forward
    And ringing their arms.

JUST ONE MORE WRONG
ECLIPSE OF THE SUN

Our knife had been drawn
　　And ready
　　To tackle any aggressive sign on the wall
　　In this city
　　Of no shame.

MEANWHILE
　　The quarreling tribes continued
　　Their endless train rides
　　Exchanging people and cattle
　　Counting fragile swamps
　　In our scattered neighborhoods.

ONLY ONE TRAFFIC light had been left
　　On the crossroad
　　Reminding us
　　We'd never been here before.

OUR CONSCIOUS VERTIGO

We've carefully observed
    From a safe distance
    The generals and hoplites
    Re-enacting
    Who knows how many times
    Their fall in the battle
    At the edge of a desert oasis
    Which had blossomed once a year in the distant past.

AFTER all
    It was up to Salvator Mundi
    To decide
    Wether they were all still going to remain in love
    Or die.

QUESTIONING IN VAIN

I know it well
    It will happen
    One ill day
    For sure
    A meteorite will disintegrate
    After crashing
    Against our heads.

TO IMAGINE it all
    Was one thing
    But knowing and feeling immortal
    Became our unnecessary lasting obsession
    While we still humbly
    Went to work.

TREES CONTINUE
TO GROW

To be honest about it
    We never expected a soft landing
    On the purple planet
    Where the radiation was so high
    And the chance of survival
    So risky.

THAT'S when we promised ourselves
    That our ancient faithful oath
    Would forever protect us
    And remind us of the possibility of renewed life
    There
    In our neighborhood
    When we fell into the sleep of the righteous
    Not far from
    The village no one ever conceived us in
    But instead
    We could notice our shallow graves immediately

Dug up in a hurry:
A stone's throw away from here.

OUR BRILLIANT
ANCESTORS

The mob surrounding the temple of Mars
    Chanted accusations
    Demanding the head of Caesar:
    But all that effort was
    To no avail.

THE DEEP SIGHS of the Vestal Virgins
    Accompanied by prayers and sad songs
    Only increased the bloodthirst within the mob
    Demanding a justice only known to them
    But completely unclear
    When it came to the decisive sentencing
    Of the heavenly court
    While the barbarians still struggled
    To cut through
    All those fratricidal conspiracies
    In our otherwise quiet suburbia.

THE LAST EFFORT

It was our usual
    Morning *salto mortale*
    In the city plagued by slumber
    Where the bells tolled once more from the start
    Announcing that something would happen there
    After all.

BUT what
    No one knew.

WE STILL STUCK to our word
    As an assurance
    For cheating time
    And being properly prepared
    For what we had been counting on:

                .   .   .

On dirges
  Our futile laments.

BEFORE THE UPRISING

It was all to do
    With the same torn up uniform
    She had worn in the picture
    Before the hanging
    We still tried to explain
    To all those willing to listen.

NO ONE KNEW how to react properly
    And that's why they all just shrugged their shoulders
    While confused postmen continued to run
    With the grenades in their bags
    Instead of love letters.

BUT WHAT WAS SO special
    About it all
    We asked ourselves
    While escaping

Behind the columns of the exiles
Hoping finally to settle somewhere.

MEN IN TROUBLE

One more bus came to a halt
    And the shadows of deserters
    Quickly jumped out
    While singing songs
    Of discouraged love.

THEY LEFT their bodies
    In the trenches and mud
    Their torn uniforms
    And letters from home
    Scattered over the bones now
    Glowing gently white in the darkness.

NAMES TO REMEMBER

Our grey heads gently swayed in the desert wind
    Surrounded by Saracen horses on all sides:
    They continued to compete across the sand
    Up and down
    Singing to our oblivion and suffering.

WHAT'S ALL this to do
    With the ending of the world
    Someone would ask
    Not knowing our wishes
    Cut down
    With the first random swing
    Of a barbarian sword.

WE ARE NOT from here
    We repeated in vain
    Lost in the last spasm
    Before rising towards our Lord.

INFECTED CIRCLES

Many had gathered there
    They hung from the branches
    Deciding to survive winter
    In the trees.

MEN WOMEN CHILDREN birds
    Knew well how they felt
    The new world will have to wait for them
    At least for another few millennia.

IN FACT this was no man's land
    And their refusal
    To fall to the ground
    And escape
    Continued to confuse us all.

BEGGING THE GODS TO
FORGIVE THE LIVING

Strange people they were
    Most of them silently
    Refusing to tell us where they came from.

ALL AROUND DARKNESS descending
    While it was too late to understand a single word they were
saying
    Only guessing
    They would all settle somewhere
    Soon
    And talking them into doing otherwise was all in vain
    Nothing more could be gained
    Because we've been trying to erase our memory too
    With not much success.

CLOSING OUR EYES FOR
ONLY A MOMENT

On both sides of the river
    Wrinkled rocks were making faces
    Expecting
    Hordes of butterflies
    To land in our wide-open mouth
    And sink us into quicksand forever.

WE WEREN'T sure
    We were the only ones who had shut our eyes for a moment
    Inhaling and exhaling bitter waters
    And noticing our ancestors suddenly
    Who never learned how to swim
    But always were ready
    To pick a good fight.

HOLY MADNESS

We wandered from bestiary to bestiary
    Praying to the Almighty
    In tongues we didn't even know we had:
    Grant us a gift of silence.

WE TRAVELED WIDE imperial roads
    Never understanding clearly
    What lurked behind those slippery rocks.

THERE WERE NO MORE caravans there
    With their tents and tamed elephants
    Only some dark angry men
    Quickly pulling bayonets from under their belts
    Cutting down snowy mountain peaks
    Even before we could reach the summit.

THIS WAS a story

Usually told around dying campfires
When memories burn to the very end
And we continue floating
In a dreamy vortex of the oncoming war of wars
Imagining
That after each gunshot
We would finally learn how to climb the melting icebergs.

CHEATING THE PAST

We drank coffee
    Not aware of the evil eye
    Observing us day and night.

IT APPEARED that the conspiracy
    Regarding the assassination of the royal couple
    Wasn't a secret after all.

A DESIRE for revenge
    Gnawing in our breast for ages
    Was enough to make us
    Completely neglect our mind
    Despite
    Various illusory miracles
    And an occasional
    Late unbeliever
    Already deceased.

SUDDEN LANDING

Did anyone suspect
    Anything
    When our curiosity had dug up
    The remains
    Of the child soldiers
    Forgotten in a nearby trench.

WE DISCOVERED them still sleeping
    With their white
    Eyes poisoned
    And their mouths
    Overgrown with thorns
    Instead of smiles.

NO NEED TO PREDICT THE FUTURE

We've cut masks out of the sacred books
    Stealing our tribe's precious words
    At the end
    Leaving them orphaned.

AMONG THE CAPPADOCIAN martyrs
    We were the only pagans:
    We promised them
    To return sooner or later
    Quickly hiding
    Our plowed faces
    In thin layers of salt.

THEY SAID we reminded them
    Of circus acrobats when they jump out at dawn.

· · ·

LATER THE YOUNG girls escorted us
    To the river
    Where we managed to wash off our transparent skin
    And escape in time.

EVEN THE MEMORIES
COULD BACKFIRE

In the café hidden behind the city walls
    Poets were carefully cutting their veins
    While at the same time inhaling open skies
    And sharing the fading lights
    With the beggars lying nearby.

IN THE MEANTIME
    We were humbly exiting the temple
    Of all our misfortunes
    Singing hymns to the useless walled-in saints
    And hitting our foreheads
    Against their tear-splattered apparitions.

WHAT COULD we remember
    When there was nothing left
    Of our broken cradle
    Scattered by the wind
    And forgetting.

. . .

WE SUDDENLY WOKE up
Letting our sabers flash
But it was already too late
When the curtain fell
And the wars ended happily.

WHEN THE SINGER GOES SILENT

She tried to hang herself in front of the mirror
    Nonchalantly throwing her hair back
    Not aware
    She would go mad in minutes:
    Her favorite song could be still heard
    On the radio.

THIS WASN'T some false pretense
    Or ruse
    Because as soon as she fell
    His body immediately relaxed
    And disintegrated instantly.

DISCIPLINE IN THE HOSPITAL

When the afternoon arrived
    We were already filled with anger
    Raging and stumbling
    Over scattered stones
    As if the Day of Resurrection
    Had already marked our inevitable defeat.

LATER WE STAYED TOO LONG
    In earthly canyons
    In the field hospitals
    Covered with leaves
    Nailed to our metal crosses and coffins.

IF THE MOTHERLAND cared for us at all
    Our names would be beautifully engraved
    In the rock face now
    Above us

But this time
We were left as orphans only
Still believing in the possible overthrow
Of our sacred oblivion.

IT WAS STILL DARK
OUTSIDE

We were humbly prostrating ourselves
    Before the mirage of a bombed-out city
    Where the dogs were the first ones to take care of themselves
    Escaping into the underground temple
    Carved out and drilled deep in the opal rock
    While the ocean tides left
    Always the same plastic bones behind
    All those scattered tumors
    Of man's neglect and perversion.

A GAP between night and day
    Grew quickly
    Turning into an extraordinary challenge
    In our suburb under the siege
    But when the slow train entered
    The skeletal remains of the local terminus
    No one disembarked
    Only uniformed guards and officers

Continued to crunch the pebbles with their boots
Hoping
Any minute
For the attack to start from the deep trenches
Somewhere nearby.

WITH NO END IN SIGHT

Everyone around us had tried stubbornly
    To persevere
    Something precious
    In the fast river
    In the canyon filled with human debris
    And the extinct species of various blue rodents.

THE SEER'S TREMBLING hand was after all
    Pointing into the right direction
    Breaking every known rule in the book
    Pushing us into a battle of sorts
    Where no one could win or live.

ONCE THE BRONZE spears had pierced our necks
    We could reveal to everyone then
    What usually takes place
    When we play a game of hiding and seek
    With the sun and moon.

OUR NATIVE LAND
AT DUSK

After the latest Armageddon
    When the Four Horses of Apocalypse
    Collided somewhere around the corner in the dark
    We found ourselves in a labyrinth
    Where the meek fateful begged for us to be rescued
    And only the innocence could save them all
    Not to fall into a trap
    Where we consciously
    Had already fallen once before.

AFTER THE VILLAGE dirges
    Gradually died down
    And the temples had emptied for the last time
    No one had any strength left
    To run
    And report the tragicomic fate
    Of all those who had survived against all odds.

          .   .   .

AND WHY WOULD anyone inform someone
    Regarding yet another ending of the world
    When in any case
    We were still getting up and lying down somehow
    For millennia
    Pretending that all was well
    And that the shadows of the heavens hanging above us
    Would shield us eventually
    From imminent self-inflicted wounds.

BUT suddenly now
    The bloodthirsty beast rightly went pale
    Losing the ground under its feet
    Before the poisonous breath
    Of the barbarian hordes
    Disturbed us again
    Behind the transparent curtains
    In the half-empty theatre.

SHOOTING HAD BEGUN ALREADY

WE MUST CONFESS to you first
    That we've gone through this before
    Several times
    Drowning in the fiery lava
    And begging the ancient Roman poet
    To rescue us
    From yet another tight spot
    Where we had become stuck
    By no fault of our own.

BEFORE DECIDING to throw

The first stone at our ancestors
We were certainly
The last ones to avoid
The anger in the colosseum.

BUT THERE WAS no going back
Despite our attempts to perform
Various gladiator exercises
Before surviving
And on our palm showing
Our pierced hearts.

WE KNOW that ancient books
Always end up in the dust
And our tongues
Free of words
Will be devoured sooner or later
By new pilgrims
Before the night swallows us all.

CONSPIRING AGAINST
OURSELVES AGAIN

A seemingly innocent column of refugees
   Crowded pedestrian crosswalks
   In that sandy landscape
   Where barbed wire and thorns
   Presented the last line
   Before the world disintegrated
   And whatever was left of it
   Sinks underground
   And falls into infinite slumber.

WHEN THE OCEANS begin to breathe hard
   And Earth starts to heave and sigh
   Under your feet
   It's time then to skip across the frontier
   And catch some other train
   Running in the opposite direction
   Of every cosmic law there is.

· · ·

THAT'S the way it is:
    You smoke and drink coffees all day long
    And laugh at night
    In the underground bars
    Where everything is fine and dandy
    Without any danger of finding yourselves again
    On the wrong side of the barricades.

SUICIDE OUT OF BOREDOM

We wasted quite a bit of time
    At dusk
    Picking sparse herbs
    Along the shore
    The weeds of forgetfulness
    Wild everywhere
    In this landscape devoid
    Of any loving-kindness.

EXHAUSTED and surprised
    After discovering sacred bones
    Buried in the bushes
    We immediately became aware that
    Our resurrection has been postponed once again
    Exactly the way the sage Vyasa had predicted
    A long time ago.

BUT IN THE end

It all comes down to that same closing verse
When the flock of birds
Wickedly ravages
Our will to live
Feeding on the scattered fragments
Of our depleted minds.

WE WOULD RATHER
ESCAPE SOMEWHERE

Even before the uprising
    The streets of our city
    Had become the only line of defense.

ALL THOSE WHO wanted a better future
    Thought they could just show up there
    And face
    The judge and jury
    Before joining the army of castaways.

THERE WAS NO MORE regret
    No sad faces before the firing squads
    Only a pagan fatalism
    It would all turn out all right
    As long as we were brave
    Starting from the beginning again
    Gnawing the irons
    And finally relaxing in the warm embrace of oblivion.

OUR PAST KNOCKS AT
THE DOOR

We didn't remember the names
    Of the ones who had lived before
    Nor were we in the mood
    To resettle their soft bones
    As far as we could
    Away from our dreams.

THE STARS WERE WELL KNOWN
    As tricksters
    Promising the light at first
    And then deceiving us in the dark
    Disappearing without a trace or sound
    As if they were never here in the past.

IN THE STREETS we observe now
    The passersby who threaten us
    They wave their hands
    Not seeing

We don't exist anymore
Because it's been well known
The witches never slept
But instead they descended into
The bed
And began to deconstruct our soul
Until another dawn broke out.

SUDDENLY

Someone knocked at the door
But we didn't dare respond.

AS WE BARELY MADE
A TURN

She squeezed the four-month-old
    Child
    Against her breast
    Smiling
    Inside the airplane
    Filled with nasty beasts
    Refusing to buckle up.

THE WRECKAGE WAS STILL BURNING
    Finding us yawning and stretching our necks
    Hoping to absorb at least some of the paleness of mother and
child
    Ready to give up
    Our belief
    In the out-of-grave existence
    At the slopes of the mountain
    Where wolves chewed the sky
    And the mountain flowers underneath the snow

Refused to blossom again.

MEANWHILE
We continue
Our flight
Dreaming of the next soft landing.

BOWING TO TYRANTS

We suffered an enlightening electric shock
    When crossing the shallow Rubicon
    While the red traffic light continued to flash
    On the same crosswalk
    Where our various fur-wearing relatives were
    Crowding
    Leaving the provinces finally
    For the distant cities
    To fulfill their insatiable hunger
    For the new neon light and exotic landscapes.

THEY WERE all in a hurry
    Not noticing
    How fast the geyser rushed upwards
    From the throat of an occasional passerby
    Like a river
    Carrying the paper boats
    Down those always dangerous streets.

                    .   .   .

WHO WAS the mob
    Cheering
    The extinction of the last
    Innocent man:
    We've been here since time immemorial
    We tell them
    But then our roots vanish
    With the speed of light
    Under the wheels
    Of the city bus.

WE WON'T ESCAPE EASILY
    From this ruined suburbia
    But at least
    We'll remember once in a while
    That
    Ordinary autumn day.

NO SIGNS OF OUR DESPAIR

WE LIVED a long time ago
    In more comfortable places
    Before becoming stuck
    In this aging
    Mausoleum
    Only to find ourselves
    Eyes closed
    But fully aware
    Everyone had forgotten us.

ACCEPTING our fate
    As it always was

Hungry and thirsty
In desperate need
Of touch and innocent
Sensual perversion
We never felt
The time abandoning us
In a silent loneliness
Of an occasional
Worthless sigh
Here and there.

ALTHOUGH THE STUDENTS of love
And their frightened lady teachers
Observed us all day long
We never paid any attention
Nor did we ever try to wake up
And break the shatter-proof glass
Pressed against us but not detected by any alarm
Or at least never expressed
The desire
For a decent revenge.

BUT ONE COLD day
We did run like bats from hell
Laughing and whistling
The hymn of the country
Which didn't exist
Anywhere anymore.

PARTICLES OF AIR

THIS WAS a picture

Clearly showing
They did everything to hang her
But to no avail.

SHE STARED at bloodless leaves
Of her homeland
Ready to take off
With the infinite will
Of one who knew where to find freedom.

UNDER A WITHERED tree
L.R. stood
In her guerilla uniform
With the gunpowder in her pockets
Ready to add her name
To the list of martyrs
With lips tightly pressed
Passing quickly
Through this world before
Taking her eternal flight
Without paying any attention
To the beasts in their helmets
Standing at attention
Unsuccessfully trying
To braid her hair
Into the shape
Of a hangman's noose.

WITHOUT REGULAR TRAFFIC

She said she wasn't from here.

ALL SHE DID WAS SIT SILENTLY by the window
    Swallowing fresh tears and fear.

NO ONE WOULD HELP her
    While the train stood idle
    Huffing and puffing
    Awaiting an occasional late passenger.

THE LOCOMOTIVE WHISTLE sounded in the ravine
    Exhaling steam in vain
    Desiring to be loved
    Lost in the reverie
    Of its interrupted
    Journey

While the wagons were still corroding
In the knee-deep snowdrifts
Filled with inert disintegration
During the eternally postponed return.

LEAVING FINALLY

It wasn't a matter anymore
    Of original sin or our wasted time
    After the swift fall through wide trenches of nothingness.

LAST TIME he dragged himself
    From the moist darkness of his room
    He never expected
    That returning home
    Would ever happen again.

HE'S BEEN PROMISED a lot in life
    Tormented or pampered
    Despite being struck by nameless ocean tides
    When all he could do was kneel
    Before her pale deathbed
    And read the words
    Of an unrepentant seer.

. . .

I WON'T LET you go
He continued to dream.

NOTICING PEOPLE

She crossed the street
　　She stumbled and flew away.

AND A LITTLE LOWER OVER there
　　Beneath the impenetrable city armor
　　There was an increasing number of those
　　Who had suffered from hunger and thirst
　　Chasing the musicians
　　Down the street
　　Whose instruments were scarred
　　By bullets and daggers
　　And not caring
　　To show any courage.

IT WASN'T a matter of
　　Simple survival
　　In the holy family nest
　　Just before the sun turned around

But about avoiding
The fact
That children were still being born unnecessarily
While passengers lay everywhere
In every corner of the train station
Scattered dead and forgotten
On wooden lacquered benches
And on crowded platforms
Where the beasts freely roamed
Not paying any attention
To those who remained awake
To sing.

FINALLY COMING TO OUR SENSES

It was a long journey
    Along these forgotten imperial roads
    With bronze helmets corroding on the way to Troy
    With the blinded hordes hiding
    Behind their thorn banners
    Always stuck on the same crossroads
    Between the barbarians and werewolves:
    How could they survive now
    Without any air
    And bread.

IT WOULD BE effortless
    To participate
    In their common history
    If no one took it
    So seriously.

www.ingramcontent.com/pod-product-compliance
Lightning Source LLC
Chambersburg PA
CBHW071922120726

48001CB00005B/1830